My Friend Rabbit

ERIC ROHMANN

SQUARE
FISH

Roaring Brook Press

For Nicholas, Ethan, and William

SQUARE
FISH

Imprints of Macmillan

MY FRIEND RABBIT. Copyright © 2002 by Eric Rohmann. All rights reserved. Printed in China by RR Donnelley Asia Printing Solutions Ltd.,
Dongguan City, Guangdong Province. For information, address Square Fish, 175 Fifth Avenue, New York, NY 10010.

Roaring Brook Press® is a registered trademark of Roaring Brook Press.
Square Fish and the Square Fish logo are trademarks of Macmillan and are used by Roaring Brook Press under license from Macmillan.

Library of Congress Cataloging-in-Publication Data Rohmann, Eric. My friend rabbit/
By Eric Rohmann   P.   cm. Summary. Something always seems to go wrong when Rabbit is around, but Mouse lets him play
with his toy plane anyway because he is a good friend. [1. Friendship—Fiction. 2. Rabbits—Fiction. 3. Mice—Fiction.] I. Title
PZ7R6413 My 2002   [E]—dc21   2002017764

Originally published in the United States by Roaring Brook Press
Square Fish logo designed by Filomena Tuosto
First Square Fish Edition: March 2007

ISBN 978-0-7613-1535-3 (Roaring Brook Press hardcover)
20 19 18 17 16 15 14

ISBN 978-0-312-36752-7 (Square Fish paperback)
20 19 18 17 16 15 14 13 12 11

LEXILE: BR

My friend Rabbit means well.
But whatever he does,
wherever he goes,

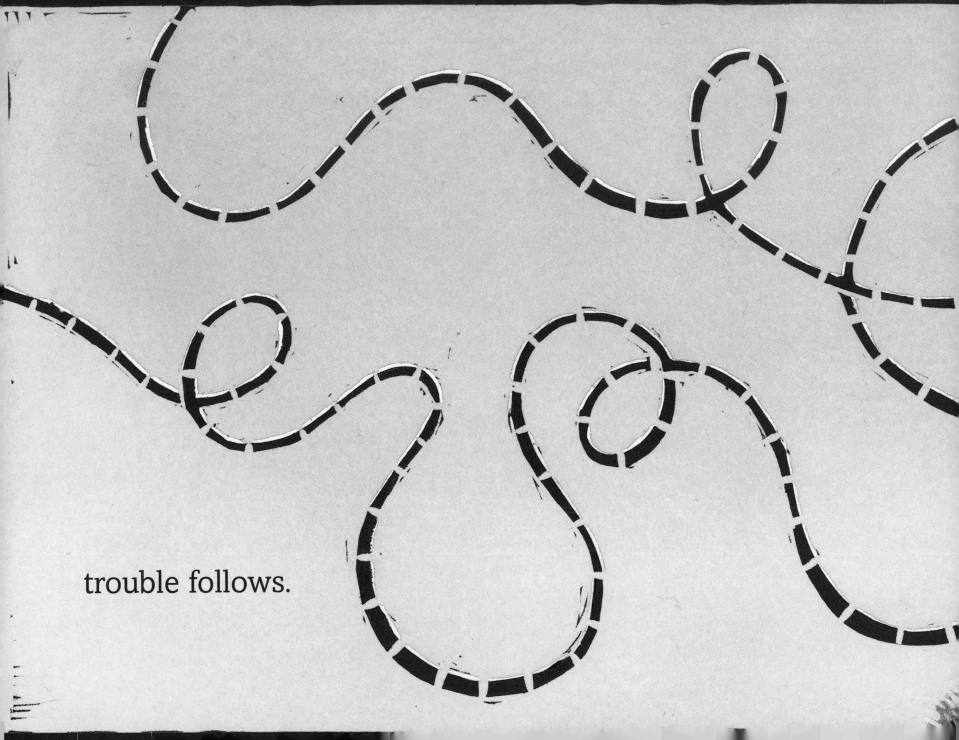

trouble follows.

"Not to worry, Mouse. I've got an idea!"

The plane was
just out of reach.
Rabbit said,
"Not to worry,
Mouse, I've
got an idea."

So Rabbit held Squirrel
and Squirrel held me . . .

but then . . .

The animals
were not
happy.

But Rabbit means well.

And he is my friend.

Even if, whatever he does,

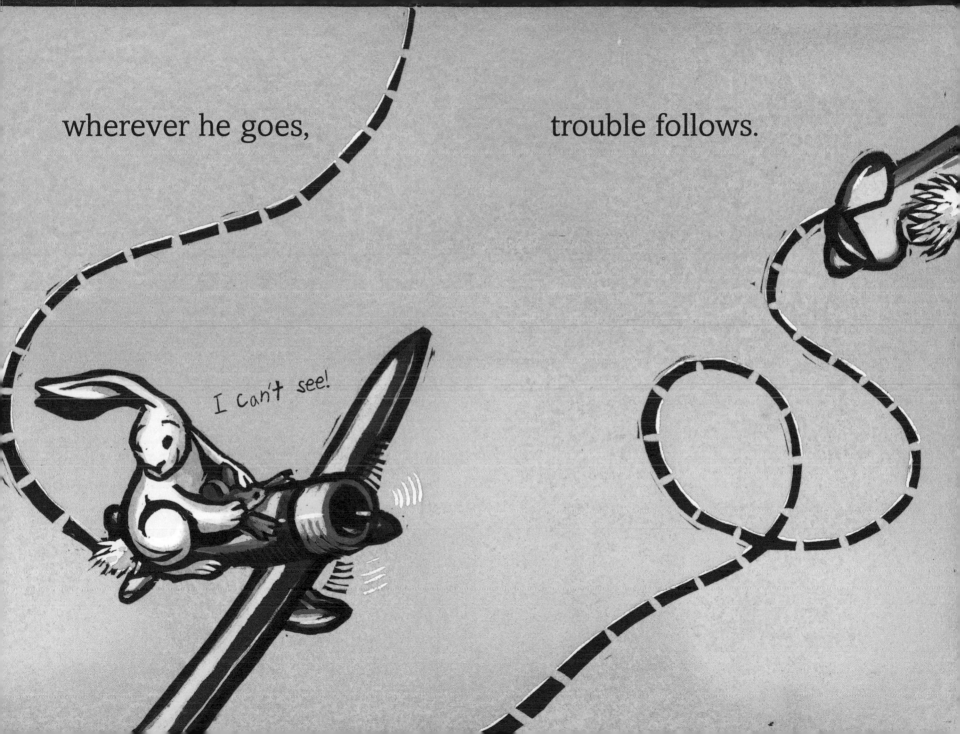

"Not to worry, Mouse,
   I've got an idea."